-HAUNTED HISTORY-

ALCATRAZ IS HAUNTED!

MARIE MORRISON

PowerKiDS press.

NEW YORK

Published in 2021 by The Rosen Publishing Group, Inc.
29 East 21st Street, New York, NY 10010

Editor: Jill Keppeler
Book Design: Rachel Rising

Portions of this work were originally authored by Ryan Nagelhout and published as *Haunted! Alcatraz.* All new material this edition authored by Marie Morrison.

Photo Credits: Cover, Matthew Slade/Shutterstock.com; Cover, pp.1-32 (background) Slava Gerj/Shutterstock.com; p. 5 Patrick Schadler/Shutterstock.com; p. 7 Ruben Martinez Barricarte/Shutterstock.com; p. 9 Maciej Bledowski/Shutterstock.com; p. 11 f8grapher/Shutterstock.com; p. 13 https://commons.wikimedia.org/wiki/File:Alcatraz_Light_citadel_Hopi.jpg; p. 15 PhotoQuest/Contributor/Getty Images; p. 17 CAN BALCIOGLU/Shutterstock.com; p. 19 Krzysztof Stefaniak/Shutterstock.com; p. 21 Joel McCartan/Shutterstock.com; p. 23 Donaldson Collection/Contributor/Getty Images; p. 24 Justin Sullivan/Getty Images News/Getty Images; p.25 Archive Photos/Stringer/Getty Images; p. 27 Arne Beruldsen/Shutterstock.com; p. 29 Anne-Marie Hartman/Shutterstock.com; p. 30 Manuela Durson/Shutterstock.com.

Cataloging-in-Publication Data

Names: Morrison, Marie.
Title: Alcatraz is haunted! / Marie Morrison.
Description: New York : PowerKids Press, 2021. | Series: Haunted history | Includes glossary and index.
Identifiers: ISBN 9781725319882 (pbk.) | ISBN 9781725319905 (library bound) | ISBN 9781725319899 (6 pack)
Subjects: LCSH: United States Penitentiary, Alcatraz Island, California--Juvenile literature. | Haunted prisons--California--Alcatraz Island--Juvenile literature.
Classification: LCC HV9474.A4 M67 2021 | DDC 365′.979461--dc23

Manufactured in the United States of America

CPSIA Compliance Information: Batch #CSPK20. For further information contact Rosen Publishing, New York, New York at 1-800-237-9932.

CONTENTS

SMALL ISLAND, BIG SHADOW

For many years, Alcatraz Island—located in San Francisco Bay off California—has captured imaginations with its generally spooky, often violent, and sometimes just plain weird history. This rocky island has been a wildlife **habitat**, a military base, an infamous prison, a protest site, and now, a famous tourist attraction and National Historic Landmark.

Some would argue, however, that the island is more than that, even now. Stories and legends about former (and current?) residents and mysterious escape attempts abound. Today, the history and fantasy of Alcatraz can be tough to separate, but either way, this small island still casts a big shadow. Step onto its rocky shores and into its dark halls and decide for yourself—is Alcatraz Island haunted?

This photograph shows Alcatraz Island as seen from San Francisco. The island is about 1.5 miles (2.4 km) off the coast.

SPOOKY STUFF

Alcatraz Island (also called "the Rock") is only about 22 acres (8.9 ha). Grand Central Terminal in New York City is more than twice as big! The railroad station covers about 48 acres (19.4 ha).

EARLY HISTORY

The first people to visit Alcatraz may have been the **indigenous** Miwok and Ohlone peoples. The Miwok and Ohlone lived around the San Francisco Bay area, although no one knows today if they used the island for anything. It's possible they camped or collected food there.

In August 1775, Spanish naval officer Juan Manuel de Ayala sailed into San Francisco Bay. He and his men started exploring the area, including the bay and its islands. He gave one island the name Isla de los Alcatraces—Spanish for "Island of the Pelicans." No one's sure which island he named, but people later transferred the name to what we now call Alcatraz. His exploration claimed the area for New Spain, which would later become Mexico.

The pelicans that lived on Alcatraz in 1775 probably were brown pelicans. These brown pelicans are shown flying past the island in modern times.

GOLD RUSH TO CIVIL WAR

By the late 1840s, with the end of the U.S.-Mexican War, Alcatraz Island (and the rest of California) became the property of the United States. Around the same time, the famous California gold rush began. In 1850, President Millard Fillmore ordered that Alcatraz and other lands in the area be used for "public purposes."

In part because of the number of gold seekers arriving in California, the U.S. Army built a fort on Alcatraz Island. This fortress, finished in 1859, had more than 100 cannons, making it very well armed. In fact, during the U.S. Civil War, it was the biggest fort west of the Mississippi River.

That war brought the next stage of Alcatraz into existence. The fort never fired its guns in a war, but it did hold prisoners.

SPOOKY STUFF

There are claims that the old Alcatraz lighthouse still appears on foggy nights. Before long, however, it vanishes again.

-A Light in the West-

Many ships wrecked along the California coastline as people traveled toward gold rush territory. In 1854, the first lighthouse on the West Coast of the United States started shining off Alcatraz Island. After the huge San Francisco earthquake of 1906 damaged this first lighthouse, engineers built a new one that still lights up the night today. Perhaps the ghosts of those gold rush shipwreck victims still seek the land even now?

Alcatraz held soldier prisoners before the Civil War, and by 1861, it was an official military prison. Then, during the war, it became home to many people who'd been arrested for treason. In 1863, an order by President Abraham Lincoln meant the government could arrest and imprison people without a trial. People who said things against the Union or in support of the Confederacy could and did find themselves serving time in the middle of the Rock—where hundreds of Union soldiers also prepared for war.

According to stories, conditions for these prisoners were fairly **brutal**. They lived in chains, trapped in a dark basement with no bathrooms, water, or heat. Is it any surprise to think that some of them might have left ghosts behind?

SPOOKY STUFF

It can be hard to find facts (as opposed to stories) about Alcatraz, but workers Daniel Pewter and Jacob Unger may have been the first two people to die on the island. The two men were crushed in a huge rockslide in 1857.

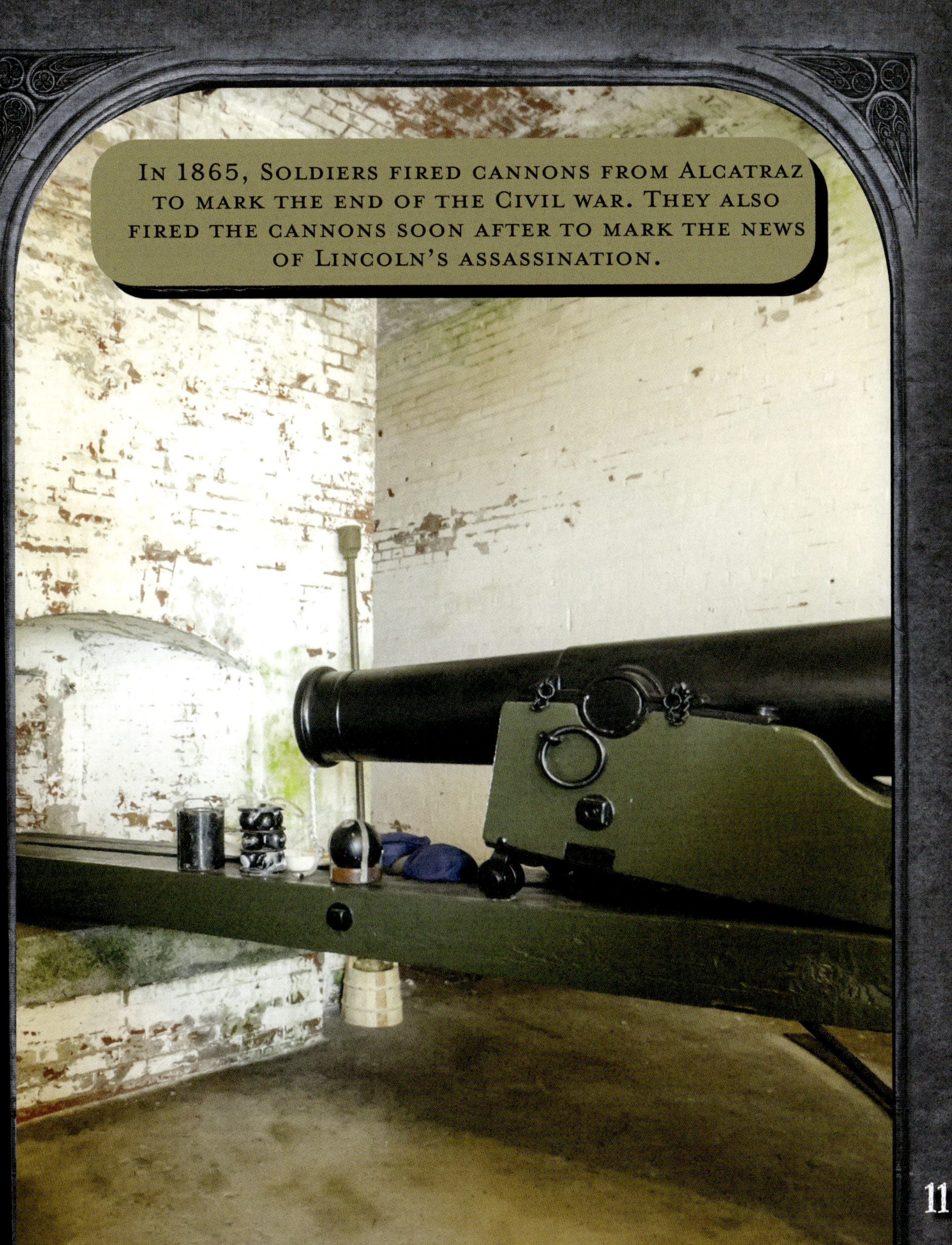

In 1865, soldiers fired cannons from Alcatraz to mark the end of the Civil War. They also fired the cannons soon after to mark the news of Lincoln's assassination.

A HISTORY OF PROTEST

Over the years, prisoners and workers built quarters for more prisoners. The population continued to rise during the Spanish-American War in 1898. By the early 20th century, Alcatraz served mostly as a **disciplinary** site for the U.S. Army.

Soldiers weren't the only prisoners, however. In 1895, the U.S. government imprisoned 19 members of the Hopi people on Alcatraz. They'd protested after the government tried to force them to use their lands in a way they didn't want and forced their children to leave for faraway boarding schools. In return, the protestors were arrested and sent to Alcatraz, where they dealt with harsh conditions and forced labor for about a year. It was just the start of a longtime tradition of the island's connection with Native Americans standing up for their rights.

No one is sure how many of the Hopi men died at Alcatraz. The government also imprisoned other Native Americans on Alcatraz. Some were executed there.

- Death on Alcatraz -

A number of people died on Alcatraz during its time as a fort. Some deaths were from disease and accidents, but some were a little more unusual. According to records of the time, Capt. William D. Dietz killed his wife on Alcatraz on January 28, 1891. He then killed himself. Later, in 1909, Sgt. Roy Ford threw Private Thomas Mullaly out a window, killing him. Ford then killed himself as well.

MAXIMUM SECURITY

Over time, the old prison on Alcatraz started to crumble. People building a new prison tore the old buildings down starting in late 1908, but they kept the old basement. The new prison rose over the old one's foundation. The U.S. military continued to use it until the early 1930s. That year, the federal government took over the island to use it as the country's first **maximum-security** prison.

After changes to make it even more secure, this facility would famously become home to some of the most dangerous **civilian** prisoners in the United States. It was meant to house people that other prisons might not contain. Alcatraz's **isolated** spot in the San Francisco Bay meant they'd be far from the rest of U.S. civilization.

ALCATRAZ WAS MEANT TO BE A PRISON FOR THE WORST OF THE WORST. SOME PEOPLE CALLED IT THE "PRISON SYSTEM'S PRISON."

THE GREAT DEPRESSION

During the Great Depression of 1929 to 1939, organized crime—groups of professional criminals who work together—soared. The federal prison on Alcatraz was, in part, a reaction to this. Some of the most famous prisoners were key organized crime figures such as Al Capone and George "Machine Gun" Kelly. The prison kept them isolated from the rest of their criminal organizations.

DOING TIME ON THE ROCK

Alcatraz was, unsurprisingly, not a fun place to live. It was considered a maximum-security and minimum-privilege, or "super max," prison. Courts and judges couldn't just sentence someone to time on Alcatraz. Prisoners went there after they'd shown themselves to be the worst troublemakers at other prisons. Most stayed on the island about five to eight years. Sometimes they returned to lower security prisons after a while.

The rules were very **strict**. For a few years, the prison inmates weren't even allowed to talk to each other, except for very brief times. Prisoners had few visitors and a tight schedule of work and meals. They couldn't receive any news of the outside world, even when they did have visitors. Conditions were worse for those who misbehaved.

Alcatraz cells only had a small place to sleep, a toilet, and cold water. Imagine spending eight years here!

Spooky Stuff

Most of the cells in Alcatraz were about 5 feet (1.5 m) by 9 feet (2.7 m). Most prisoners could stretch out their arms and touch either side of their cell.

LIFE AND DEATH BY THE NUMBERS

For all the spooky stories about Alcatraz, relatively few people actually died there during the island's time as a maximum-security site. Fifteen people died from illnesses, while five killed themselves. Eight people were killed by others.

Contrary to some stories, however, no one was executed at Alcatraz while it was a federal prison. The government didn't send prisoners with a death sentence there, and it transferred those who received such a sentence while on the island.

Of course, Alcatraz is also known for its escape attempts. According to the U.S. government, during the time the federal prison was open, there were 14 escape attempts involving 36 inmates. Of those inmates, 23 men were caught and eight died. Five disappeared—but no one knows for sure what happened to them.

THE PRISON ON ALCATRAZ HAD A **MORGUE**, BUT NO ONE USED IT. THOSE WHO DIED ON THE ISLAND WERE SENT TO THE MAINLAND.

SPOOKY STUFF

THE AVERAGE POPULATION OF THE ALCATRAZ FEDERAL PRISON WAS 260 MEN. THE GREATEST NUMBER OF PRISONERS DURING ALCATRAZ'S TIME AS A FEDERAL PRISON WAS 302.

-MYTH BUSTED?-

One of the most famous Alcatraz escape attempts took place in 1962. Inmates Frank Morris and John and Clarence Anglin took off on a raft made from raincoats. No one ever saw the three men again, although there are many stories about them. In 2003, the TV show *MythBusters* tried to repeat the men's escape to see if they could have survived. It concluded that they could have!

THE DEADLIEST DAY

While the guns of Alcatraz never fired when the island was a fort, an event now called the Battle of Alcatraz did take place in May 1946. Prisoners Marvin Hubbard, Bernard Coy, and Joseph Cretzer worked together to get a guard's keys and got into the prison's gun storage. They released many other inmates and killed two guards, although they never made it out of the prison.

People gathered across the water in San Francisco to watch as the island lit up with gunfire and explosions. "The island was a ring of fire in the night," one observer wrote. Hubbard, Coy, and Cretzer died when guards and U.S. Marines attacked the cellblock to retake it. Two other inmates died as punishment for their role, or part, in the escape attempt.

Visitors have said they can smell smoke in the Cellblock C laundry room, even though there's no fire.

-Cellblock C-

Some stories tell that the hallway in Cellblock C where Hubbard, Coy, and Cretzer died is haunted. People report hearing loud noises, voices, and the sound of people running. Some say they saw images of men in uniforms. In fact, those who believe in ghosts say it's one of the most haunted sites on the island. Even the laundry room in the cellblock is said to be haunted!

PRISONERS

Some of the inmates at Alcatraz were very famous men. Some were relatively unknown. The prisoners all had one thing in common—they were all known for breaking the rules or trying to escape other prisons. Most met their match in Alcatraz. In fact, gangster Al "Scarface" Capone reportedly told a warden, "Looks like Alcatraz has got me licked." Capone had been well known at other prisons for bribing guards and working the system, but he didn't get away with it at the Rock.

The prison's inmates over the years included Capone, George "Machine Gun" Kelly, James "Whitey" Bulger, Robert Stroud (called the Birdman of Alcatraz), and Alvin "Creepy" Karpis. Many of them had done horrible things during their criminal careers, including murder, robbery, kidnapping, and brutal attacks.

SPOOKY STUFF

THE WATERS AROUND ALCATRAZ ISLAND ARE FILLED WITH SHARKS. HOWEVER, MOST OF THEM ARE SMALL SHARKS THAT DON'T CARE TO ATTACK PEOPLE. THE PRISONERS PROBABLY DIDN'T KNOW THIS, THOUGH!

CAPONE'S GANG PULLED OFF THE INFAMOUS ST. VALENTINE'S DAY **MASSACRE** IN 1929. HIS MEN SHOT DOWN A GROUP OF UNARMED RIVAL GANG MEMBERS.

-CREEPY!-

Alvin Karpis, known as "Creepy" for his strange smile, had the longest stay at Alcatraz while it was a federal prison. Karpis was an inmate from August 1936 to April 1962. He was best known for being the leader of the Karpis-Barker gang, which killed, kidnapped, and robbed people for years during the 1930s. During his time at Alcatraz, however, he never tried to escape.

Many of the ghost stories of Alcatraz refer to general visions, sounds, or feelings. Some people have reported hearing screams, gunshots, the jingling of keys, sobbing and moaning, or whistling. Others have said they've seen a "thing" with glowing eyes or ghostly images of prisoners or guards.

However, some of the stories pinpoint specific prisoners. Al Capone played the banjo in the prison band, and visitors have reported hearing a banjo near his cell—or in the shower room, where he supposedly practiced. Karpis's ghost has been rumored to hang out near the kitchen, and George Kelly's ghost apparently prefers the church—or so the stories say. People also say they've heard Robert Stroud, the so-called Birdman of Alcatraz, whistling to birds that aren't there.

-The Birdman-

Robert Stroud, made famous in part by the 1962 movie *The Birdman of Alcatraz,* was an inmate at Alcatraz for 17 years. While in prison in Kansas for murder, he started studying birds and raised canaries in his cell. However, after he was transferred to Alcatraz in 1942, he wasn't allowed to keep birds—despite the nickname the movie (which was largely fiction) gave him.

Actor Burt Lancaster played Stroud in *The Birdman of Alcatraz*. He was nominated for an Academy Award.

CELLBLOCK D

There were four cellblocks in Alcatraz, and many of the prison's ghost stories seem to focus on Cellblock D. This block of 42 cells held inmates who'd broken the rules. The cells were a bit bigger than the regular cells, in fact, but the prisoners there had to stay in them 24 hours a day. They didn't have the few privileges other inmates did. Six of those cells, the solitary **confinement** cells, didn't have any light. Prisoners named them "the Hole."

Visitors have said they've felt cold spots or feelings of panic in the Hole. One story says that an inmate locked in one of those cells started screaming that something was in there with him—and that he was found dead the next day! There are no prison records of this, however.

CELL 14D IS SUPPOSEDLY THE MOST HAUNTED OF ALCATRAZ'S CELLS.

STORIES VS. REALITY

The federal prison on Alcatraz closed in 1963, and all its prisoners were moved elsewhere. Today, the site is part of the Golden Gate Recreation Area, and many tourists visit it every year. They look and listen for the ghosts of Alcatraz and learn the history of this spooky island.

However, while the island (and its residents) definitely had a creepy side, the true history of Alcatraz prison isn't quite as brutal as some books and movies **portrayed** it. In fact, some inmates wanted to go there! Every inmate had his own cell and the food was better than that at other prisons. Prisoners who followed the rules had privileges including movies, books, and magazines. Sometimes they could have visitors.

VISITORS CAN STILL SEE SIGNS OF THE NATIVE AMERICAN PROTESTERS AT ALCATRAZ TODAY.

From November 1969 to June 1971, **activists** protesting the U.S. government's treatment of Native Americans occupied Alcatraz Island. They wanted to use the land as a school, cultural center, and museum. At one point, more than 600 people were living there. However, a fire burned down a number of the former prison's buildings, conditions got worse, some original activists had to leave, and the protest eventually ended.

THE TALES CONTINUE

It's easy to visit Alcatraz today—and it's much easier to leave! Ferries take people to the island right from Pier 33 in San Francisco. The National Parks Service runs the park, and there are no actual ghost tours. However, you can take a nighttime tour during which guides show you around and tell the stories of this island, its history, and its inmates.

Whether you believe in ghosts or not, you can peek into a cell in "the Hole," study the island's rocky shores and imagine daring and deadly escape attempts, and maybe even hear about life in the prison from a former inmate. Decide for yourself whether Alcatraz is haunted!

More than 1,500 inmates stayed at Alcatraz over the federal prison's time there. Do some of them remain?

GLOSSARY

activist: Someone who acts strongly in support of or against an issue.

brutal: Very cruel or harsh.

civilian: A person not on active duty in the military.

confinement: The act of confining, or keeping someone or something in a place.

disciplinary: Meant to correct or punish bad behavior.

habitat: The natural home for plants, animals, and other living things.

indigenous: Living naturally in a particular region.

isolated: Located in a place that is separate from others.

massacre: The violent killing of many people.

maximum: The highest amount possible.

morgue: A place where dead bodies are kept.

portray: To show as.

strict: Absolute, kept with great care.

INDEX

WEBSITES

Due to the changing nature of Internet links, PowerKids Press has developed an online list of websites related to the subject of this book. This site is updated regularly. Please use this link to access the list: www.powerkidslinks.com/haunted/alcatraz